"I could feel a smile on my face as the first chapter ended and I read on to find the journey had only just begun- a harrowing tale. And very useful for survivors. There was clarity for little bunnies everywhere that didn't ignore the complexities of trauma."

-Kelly Baas
LCPC

*"**Tijabab** speaks to a range of both personal and relational dynamics through a combination of sensitive, direct, and playful metaphors. I felt like I was treating my inner child to an insightful story time about "grown folks business". **Tijabab** is all of us in one way or another; should we choose to honestly look in the mirror and accept what we see."*

-Jenni Graham
Art Therapist LCAT, ATR-BC, MPS

"...Clemons-Hopkins has so creatively made use of a standard fable style of writing...a protective necessity as the author dives into a very authentic portrayal of domestic violence.

"...Tija's story reflects a growing movement to share our stories so that others will know they are not alone."

D1445028

i

(This Is Just Another Book About Bunnies)

TIJABAB
[TEE-juh-baab]
A Fable for Grown-Ups about Fear and Freedom

Carl Clemons-Hopkins

Illustrations by Chris Bresky

ISBN: 978-0-692-16975-9

For all who have survived.

Thrive.

Dedicated to Love.

And also to my Phenomenal Brotha. You answer when I call. Thank you.

Please, go back to sleep :)

CONTENTS

Foreward

When Carl asked me to write the foreword to his book I immediately thought, "*Me? Are you sure?*" even though my mouth responded 'Yes'. In truth, I didn't feel qualified enough to lend my words, my voice to something he was so deeply passionate about. I didn't want to be the person who dropped the ball or screwed it up. I wanted him to succeed and I didn't want to be the person whose artistic inadequacies got in the way of his success.

What if what I write isn't good?

What if he doesn't like it?

What if people read it and hate it- will that sabotage his book?

What if I suck as a writer?

What if!

What if!

What if!

And then, it hit me; I'm wrestling with the same fears Tijabab conquers in this book. This tiny, genderless bunny digs deep to choose courage over comfort. It embraces it and leans into fear with abandon. In short, it chooses purpose over paralysis.

Fear paralyzes.

It lies to us and tricks us into stepping out of alignment of who we really are and who we're meant to be. It seduces us into settling for the safety of familiar comfort instead of the liberation that accompanies foreign freedom. We're often seduced by what we believe to be rational hesitation when really, it's fear in disguise.

How do we conquer fear?

To be honest, I don't think fear is something to be conquered. For me, I think fear is something to be comforted. Fear is a counselor, a guide, an aid to help you keep the risks in perspective. However, in order to stay in alignment with who we want to become, we must prioritize our purpose over fear. We must be kind to our fears. We must tell our fears:

"Hey Fear,

I know you're there and I know you're afraid. I'm scared too. But I'm here now and you don't have to sit in the driver's seat anymore. I'll take care of both of us. Thank you for being here and reminding me how much I care about this thing. But it's okay now, you're safe. If you like, you can be my navigator. I'll let you hold the compass and you keep pointing us toward risk and truth. I'll be happy to follow your directions on which paths you think are scariest, but unfortunately, I can't let you drive. I know a better way of getting to where we both want to go: freedom. And sometimes, most times, that freedom is on the other side of the scariest parts.

Thank you for listening fear and thank you for being my friend. We're in this thing together."

If a tiny, genderless rabbit can find courage larger than itself to step heart first into freedom, then why can't I?

What the hell.

Here goes everything.

Lee Edward Colston II

Actor & Playwright

"I'll tell you what freedom is to me. No fear."

-Nina Simone

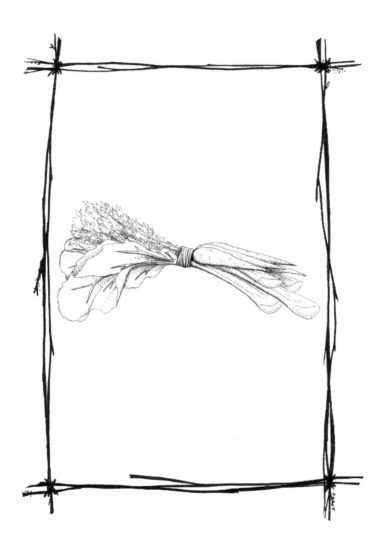

Chapter One

Fear will fucking kill you if you let it.

There once was a bunny named Tijabab, and it was a cute, little, genderless bunny with beautifully soft fur. Tija was born with a bit of a gift. The best way to explain it is that Tija was very sensitive to how others were feeling and could sometimes see another bunny's inner emotions. Additionally, Tija was a very honest little bunny, almost to a fault. Tija's parents were explicitly clear on how they felt about lying, and Tija upheld that standard just as high as it could. This made growing up particularly challenging for Tija. It seemed to always be the last one to learn the "older bunny things that all older bunnies seem to know," and much of that had to do with when little bunnies started to get better at bending the Truth. Sadly, little Tija did not quite grasp that skill.

The one thing Tija simply adored was playing make-believe. It had a truly remarkable imagination, and was convinced that if it got really, really, really good at make-believe, maybe it could comprehend what was going on in the real world. The real world can be a frequently frightening place for a cute little bunny, so Tija dedicated itself to make-believe and found safety when lost in the worlds of its own imagination. Sometimes, when Tija worked really, really hard to pretend, it would feel no Fear. Occasionally, other little bunnies would also be in that fearless make-believe space with Tija- cute little fearless bunnies in a room or outside. It was a beautiful thing to behold.

Fear was a big thing with Tija- a really big thing. Tija's entire life was plagued with night terrors, which made it see Fear as anything that interrupted rest with visions that caused worry, vexation, panic, and ultimately, terror. These night terrors were not "monsters-under-the-bed" type of events for Tija; these were depths of darkness and frights of terrifically perfect evil such that Satan himself would gouge his eyes out with hot coals before enduring another soul- sheering moment of agony in their very presence! So tormenting were Tija's night terrors that they sometimes caused Tija to violently destroy its bedroom in a half- dream fit of fright, breaking furniture, hurling toys, and tearing through everything in its path to flee its slaughterer! Often Tija would wake up with the taste of blood in its throat from screams, or find itself mired down to the bed by its own vomit, its stomach ravished from the dream battle.

One night after yet another sleeping attack, Tija's parents raced into Tija's room, terrified themselves that their cute little bunny would be its own young ruin! One bunny parent, Bab, would run and fetch a cold wet cloth, while the other parent, Big T, desperately tried to still Tija's little bunny body while also trying to not cause more harm. After Big T was sure Tija knew it was awake, albeit still quite scared, Bab would put the cold cloth to Tija's head. The cooling sensation was soothing to Tija and to its still storming

stomach. This was the day Big T had enough.

After Bab left to get Tija some warm water,

Big T sat down in the chair next to the bed. "Tija,"

it said, "I Love you. I Love you very, very much."

Big T drew a deep breath before continuing. "This

has to stop. Medicine hasn't helped, doctors don't

know what to do, and this is the third guardrail

you've broken this summer!" It paused for a

moment, truly unsure of what to say, until it knew

what to say. "Tijabab... I Love you and I need you

to know that this is nothing but Fear. Fear is not of

Good. Good gives us things that make us feel

happy and safe, not afraid. And, Tija," it continued,

"I need you to know that Fear can only kill you if

you let it. Do not let it. No matter what happens in

your cute little bunny life, do not give space to Fear."

"But what do I do when this happens again?!" cried a distraught and petrified Tija.

"Well," Big T replied, "You cannot control when or where you will see Fear, but when you do, you just stand up, breathe, and say, 'Fear! You get the fuck outta here!' You say it as mean and as loud as you want, and as many times as you need until Fear just has to leave. Go ahead! Try it!"

Tija was a bit confused by this advice but also very amused at Big T's choice of language. Big T stood Tija up on the bed and said, "Now stand up tall, Tija."

Tija did.

"Take a deep breath."

Tija did.

"Say, 'Fear!'"

"Fear!" Tija's little voice squeak-yelled.

Big T fought hard to hide its smile. "You get the fuck outta here!"

"You get the-" Tija froze. In all of its seven years it never thought it would be able to curse in the house, let alone use the biggest curse word it knew, and especially not with a parent.

"Go ahead, Tija," Big T nudged, "Fear is the only thing you're allowed to be this mean to."

Tija took another deep breath. "...YOU GET THE FUCK OUTTA HERE, FEAR!! I MEAN IT!! YOUGETDAFUCKOUTAHE-YAAAAAAAH!!!"

Bab bolted into the bedroom. "Tija!" it screamed in shock. "I will not abide cussin' in this house!"

"It's OK!", Big T said, laughing, "We are getting rid of Tija's night terrors." Tija was beaming with delight, simply beaming. It had learned its first spell!

Later that night, after Tija's parents straightened up the room and got Tija all cleaned up, Big T stood Tija up on the bathroom sink facing the mirror, looked Tija in the eye, and said, "You are gonna beat this Fear. I know you are. You are gonna get somewhere and be somebunny, and you cannot let Fear stop you. Understand?"

Tija understood as much as a cute little seven-year-old bunny could. "Yes." it said.

The night terrors did not stop. But their power decreased as Tija's spell skills increased until, eventually, many years later, Tija was able to smell the Fear even before it showed itself in the night. Tija would simply open its eyes and say "No."

Young Tija

Chapter Two
The body will reflect the Spirit.

Between having make-believe and the Spell to Send Fear Away, Tijabab felt like a seven-year-old boss-ass bitch. One truly could not tell this bunny anything whatsoever. Why, as far as little Tija was concerned, the rain didn't even fall on its head! That's how joyful this bunny was pretty much all the time. Tija woke up with a smile on its face and a song in its heart each and every morning. It greeted the morning and every other bunny in its world with glee and delight. This soft little bunny was severely cute, and everybunny that saw Tija couldn't help but smile. On the street, at the store, at school- Tija was just that cute of a little bunny.

Big T and Bab were, of course, glad their bunny was such a happy bunny, but they worried about how it would handle certain realities of the world. They did not want to ever do anything to break Tija's Spirit, so they decided the best way for Tija to learn about the world was by making education absolutely paramount. Books. Books. Books, books, books. Books. Everybunny! Books on anatomy, ecology, astronomy, books written by great bunnies of all fur colors. Old books, new books, red books, cerulean magazines- if the library was a bar and books were liquor, Tija would have died from alcohol poisoning years ago! But, as Bab would often tell an often complaining Tija, "Baby, nobunny ever died from reading too much. Now, write me three pages on what the story was about."

As time went on, something peculiar began to happen. Tija was still ever so joyful, and triumphant. It was getting smarter, which made its parents happy. It was getting bigger and stronger, which makes all little bunnies happy. Everything was going exceedingly well for young Tija. Except, occasionally, Tija started to see some things. Tija started to see some things it only saw in its dreams. The first few times Tija saw this, it thought, *Bab says that nothing in those dreams were real. They cannot be real!* Nevertheless, Tija was beginning to see Fear in the faces of certain adult bunnies when Tija smiled at them on the street. *Why didn't they smile back? They always smile back. Everybunny smiles back!*, Tija thought. But certain bunnies not only didn't smile back, there were actual traces of Fear in their eyes as they hurried away. Tija could not comprehend this.

Things were even more peculiar at the store. Tija was utterly adorable in the shopping cart seat; Bab would laugh and play with Tija while grocery shopping, and other bunny parents greeted them with smiles and marveled at Tija's beautifully soft fur. Sure, Tija was getting too big for the seat now and the cart proper needed to have room for groceries, but Bab and Tija could just push the cart together, holding paws, and still laugh and play. But certain adult bunnies did not smile when they would pass, and Tija could see the Fear in their eyes too.

The same occurred with certain teachers at school. Moreover, all kinds of older bunnies at school had Fear in their eyes when Tija would smile and be friendly towards them, but they would be laughing. This quite perplexed Tija. *How? How can they laugh with Fear in their eyes? They are laughing, so they must be happy; and happy comes from Good...but Big T said Good doesn't give Fear...*

Tija truly did not know what to do when this would happen. However, after a while, Tija realized it really didn't like seeing so many glimpses of Fear. So, at nine-and-a-quarter-years old, Tija figured it was best to not smile when it was passing people on the street or at the store, and it should definitely not smile too much at school.

However, this was hard for Tija because it kept looking at other bunnies- not smiling, of course, but looking to see if maybe the Fear had gone away from their eyes. This search caused Tija's thoughts to shift. *What are you doing, Teej? All that learning and all of those books and you're growing up to be a stupid bunny that just stares at rabbits all day? You are just... you know what it is? Yeah, you're getting too big, way too quickly. Yeah, Teej, you should try to look...smaller, if you can. That way, everybunny doesn't have Fear in their eyes when they look at you. Listen, bun, I know you think you're a cute little bunny, but I gotta tell ya, you're not exactly little. Sure, you're young, but ya ain't little. And, honestly, I know Bab says you're cute, but that's just what a parent says and you can't believe that's True. You're just a bunny. A big nine-year-old fluffy bunny. I only want to make this whole thing easier for ya, Teej. If you stay out of the way and kinda keep your head down, maybe you won't see as much Fear.* And with that thought, Tija learned its second spell. Sometimes this spell made Tija's growing bunny body hurt, but it always tried very hard to keep its head low and curve its back to look less big. Tija was sure to stay out of the way and avoid eye contact with other bunnies so it didn't have to see Fear. But sadly, with this spell, Tija began to see traces of Fear in its own eyes. Tija hated looking at itself in the mirror and would seldom smile in pictures.

And the next time they went to the store, Tija stopped holding Bab's paw.

O.G.B.

Chapter Three

Just because Fear is there, doesn't mean you gotta stare at that shit.

While the Fear-Avoidance Spell was

occasionally painful and burdensome for Tija,

there was always a reprieve in make-believe. This

Joy was still very much a part of Tija's life and

while make-believe still made Tija feel fearless,

getting to that fearless feeling proved to be more

difficult lately- not impossible, just slightly harder

than before. Regardless of this fact, Tija's Spirit

truly soared during make-believe, and as it

continued to grow up, Tija found this was often the

only thing it wanted to do. This made Tija's

parents quite happy. Big T was happy because,

although this wasn't necessarily what it thought its child would naturally go toward, this instilled discipline and dedication and kept Tija out of the kind of trouble other young bunnies found themselves in. Bab was pleased because, although it was unsure if its child would actually be any good at this, make-believe made Tija stand up a little straighter, speak up a little more, and have a more defined sense of pride. In the end, as long as Tija was striving for excellence, it really didn't matter to Big T and Bab what Tija did.

So, when the time came for a now young adult Tija to decide what it wanted to do with its life, the choice was clear and very much supported: Tija would turn its make-believe adventures into reality for others to see and enjoy-

Tija would become a creator. Several weeks before Tija was to depart for creator training, Tija's parents threw a party for their little bunny, and all of Tija's Family was there.

And those rabbits had a terribly good time!

O.G. Bunny, Tija's grandbunny, was Tija's most favorite bunny. That night, O.G.B. and Tija found themselves alone outside under the stars, a little ways away from the party. O.G.B. had acquired quite a bit of party punch that evening and was in a gloriously delightful humor. In the midst of its delightfulness, it found the capacity to tell Tija this: "TJ, I want you to look at me. Look at me, rabbit!" Tija did so. "What do you see?"

"I see you, O.G.B.!", Tija said, laughing, as O.G.B. had allowed Tija a small amount of party punch as well.

"And I see you, TJ. I'm damn proud of you, young rabbit. You've grown up to become a damn good young bunny. Now, I want you go on to that creator school place you goin' to and-" it paused. It breathed. It belched loudly. "I want you to go be yourself. You understand me, rabbit?"

Tija understood as much as a seventeen-year-old bunny could. "I will, O.G.B.," said Tija. "I Love you."

"I Love you too, TJ," replied O.G.B. as it half hugged/ half leaned on Tija in order to stay upright, and then it stumble-waddled back to the party.

Tija was unsure what prompted this brief episode with O.G.B., but was glad of the occurence because Tija saw more than Love or pride in O.G.B.'s eyes- Tija didn't see a trace of Fear. Not even a speck of it! Furthermore, Tija was amazed by the fact that O.G.B.'s eyes with no Fear could look into Tija's eyes, which were almost always full of Fear, and not be afraid. Even more confounding than this, how was O.G.B. able to have no Fear in its eyes and look at Fear in Tija's eyes, and in doing so, make Tija less afraid? Somehow, O.G.B.'s brief celebratory conversation made Tija feel encouraged, less alone, and safe. Perhaps it was the party punch, perhaps it was the cool breeze on the warm night, but Tija felt

Secure- for the first time in quite some time,

genuinely Secure. This made Tija happy. This also

made Tija wonder if it could do what O.G.B. did

and make other bunnies feel Secure.

Tija flew straight past the party to its room

to figure out the Security Spell. *Alright. What*

exactly did O.G.B. do? It looked at me with no

Fear, saw my Fear, and...and what? What made me

feel happy and Secure? It saw my Fear; why didn't

it recoil or hide like I do?

Tija couldn't quite figure it out, until it

figured it out. *O.G.B. looked at me without Fear,*

saw my Fear, but chose to... O.G.B. didn't focus on

the Fear! O.G.B. didn't focus on the Fear, it

focused on me! Yes! That's what I'll do at creator training, and that's how I'll make new Friends who enjoy make-believe as much as I do! If I see Fear in anybun's eyes, I won't focus on that, I'll focus on the bunny!

Tija was smiling a smile it hadn't smiled in nearly ten years. The Security Spell may not just be Tija's ticket to figuring out how to survive creator training; it may also be a way for Tija to feel the way it did when it was a cute little bunny.

Tija zoomed down the stairs to try out the new spell. It would still see various levels of Fear in the eyes of other bunnies, but it would make itself keep searching. *What else is there? What else can I focus on?* The search forced Tija to listen;

not only to what a bunny was saying, but to what else it saw in the bunny's eyes. After all that listening, Tija would have to respond. This caused more listening. With all this listening and responding, Tija found it didn't have time to focus on Fear. Furthermore, Tija started to notice less Fear in the other bunny the more it listened. Tija also began to feel less afraid.

During these spell experiments in the following days and weeks, Tija found itself doing something it hadn't done in years: looking somebunny in the eye and smiling. Big T and Bab were pleasantly surprised by the Tija that now descended the stairs in the morning. This Tija stood up tall, greeted you warmly, and listened to what you had to say. This Tija laughed out loud and made others laugh out loud. This new Tija was just a hoot-and-a-half and a one-bunny festival of conviviality! It found itself using the Fear-Avoidance Spell less and less, though the spell was still necessary in instances where the Fear was too great. Still, Tija very seldom used it to the point of pain anymore. Tija was here and ready to go everywhere!

Armed with the Fear-Avoidance Spell and the Security Spell, Tijabab felt ready to take on creator training and the world!

Tob

Chapter Four

Toxicity = Fear + Power (part 1)

As Tijabab entered early adulthood, it grew to realize certain things about itself. Now, most assume that all bunnies like carrots. That is seen as "normal" in most depictions of bunnies since the dawn of time. And while this is True for many bunnies, to assume that all bunnies care for carrots is, at best, silly.

Yes, many bunnies like carrots, but one must know that bunnies can delight in a whole spectrum of deliciousness! Some enjoy carrots. Some enjoy rhubarb. Some enjoy carrots and rhubarb. Some very well do not. Some enjoy tasty morsels that care to be called neither carrots nor rhubarb. And that is all right. If all bunnies involved in the meal are adults, and they are all excitedly agreeable to what is on the table, and nobun is getting hurt, it is truly all right. As for Tija, it liked rhubarb. Tija tried carrots and rather enjoyed carrots, but it was rhubarb that delivered a most delightful and definitively divine dining experience! And happily, most of the bunnies at creator training were wonderfully accepting of all tastes.

Creator training was the most exciting place Tija had ever seen in its entire life. Full of wonder and discovery, Tija soon began to thrive in this strange new place. It started making new Friends who were brilliant and fascinating, and shared the same passion for make-believe. Tija was being challenged every day at training and often felt most of its energy was spent just trying to keep up. But despite the occasional setbacks, Tija was still thrilled to be there and determined to be its very best. It was going to get somewhere and be somebunny, and this was the place to learn how!

Not only was Tija's Spirit thriving, but there was also quite a bit of activity brewing in Tija's Heart. There was this other bunny, Tob. Tijabab was perfectly mad about Tob. Tija was fully enamored by Tob's passion and zeal, its beautiful soft fur, its stunning bunny eyes, and nose, and whiskers and just everything! Tob was also quite fond of Tija, but neither bunny was brave enough to tell the other.

After some time, Tija grew frustrated with its growing affection for Tob being constantly at war with its nervousness to confess it. Tija often dreamt about what it would be like to have a meal with Tob -more than just a meal, Tija wanted a whole life with Tob. But, after all the time spent with Tob at creator training, Tija didn't even know if Tob liked rhubarb! Tija figured that the best way to know more about Tob was to simply get to know more about Tob. So, that became Tija's mission: get to know Tob.

This mission proved to be more difficult than Tija expected, however, because whenever conversations began to go past a certain point, Tija would begin to see more Fear in Tob's eyes. But this didn't stop the courageous young Tija; it would simply employ the Security Spell and look past Tob's Fear and see what else was there. The spell worked- slowly at first, but then more and more Tija would see Tob's beauty and complexity, and much to Tija's surprise, Tob would do the same. Until finally, one warm summer night, Tija and Tob found themselves fearlessly staring into each other's eyes.

And then, rhubarb. Wonderful, delicious rhubarb!

Tija and Tob planned to meet the following day and Tija practically floated to Tob's flat, and Tob greeted Tija as if it too had been floating. The subsequent weeks were filled with floating and rhubarb and such was their beautiful excitement about each other that their Friends began to take notice. This initially gave Tija and Tob some pause, but Tija got over that quickly as it had never known this kind of happiness and figured this must come from Good! Tob, however, did not quite think this way.

Everybunny's Fear is a little bit different. Yes, all Fear is Fear, but it can manifest itself differently from bunny to bunny depending on how strong it is. Though Tija ran away from Fear at a very young age, the lessons it learned from Big T and Bab, combined with the spells learned in the past twenty years, caused Tija to face Fear a lot more often. Tob, however, had different experiences with Fear in its life; so when Tob felt Fear about being with Tija, Fear caused Tob to do odd things like quickly distance itself from Tija when other bunnies went by, ridicule Tija simply for enjoying rhubarb (even though Tob clearly also enjoyed rhubarb), or allow its fur to be soft when alone with Tija but try to roughen its fur when around other bunnies.

Over time, Tob's Fear began to ebb and flow so much that it began to move beyond the point of Tob's control. Tob's Fear began to gain power and self-control, so much self-control that it soon learned how to hide from Tija when Tija looked into Tob's eyes. So when Tob saw Tija, Tob's Fear would cover itself in clever disguises like sarcastic put-downs or mockery or humiliation- at times, even insults.

Tija would be very confused by this. This was nothing like what Tija used to see in Tob's eyes. *What am I doing wrong? How can we decrease each other's Fear one moment, and in the next, Tob increases my Fear with all these things I've never seen before?*

As the months turned to years, it seemed Tob clearly wanted more than just rhubarb with Tija, yet Tija was dodging Tob's tantrums every other moment, and that did not make Tija feel happy at all. And what's worse, when Tija looked at itself in the mirror, it started to see more Fear in its own eyes. *Maybe I'm not trying hard enough.* Tija thought. *Clearly I'm not- Tob told me. OK. Let's figure this out. I love Tob and Tob loves me; it said so. Actually, I think Tob is getting a little annoyed with you asking it to 'say so' so often.* Tija's thoughts began to shift. *I get it, Teej, you are not sure why Tob loves you when it can put you down and mock you, but can you really blame Tob? You're a lot. Maybe chill a bit. Alright, we need to bring this Fear level down. You can't be out here looking afraid, Teej. You're a grown-up now- time to act like it. Here's what ya do: you are going to be perfect! I mean, really perfect. If you always say the right thing around Tob and don't do any of the things that annoy Tob and make sure everything around Tob is perfect, then Tob can't do any of the things that hurt you because it will be happy. And you will be happy because Tob is happy and you love Tob and Tob loves you! Just be excellently perfect.*

The next day, Tija tried the Spell of Perfection. Later that day, Tija failed at the Spell of Perfection.

That was the first day Tob hit Tija. And that night, Tija decided to start reemploying the Fear-Avoidance Spell.

Snow

Chapter Five

Toxicity = Fear + Power (part 2)

Snow was a bunny whose Family came from far away, where they spoke a different language and bunnies looked a bit different than the bunnies did where Tija was from. However, like Tija, Snow grew up with a great eagerness for make-believe, mostly because this curbed Snow's Fear of being judged for being a different-looking, different-sounding bunny. Make-believe made Snow feel safe, and it always sought to help others feel safe in any situation. Snow was cool. Some bunnies are not cool with other bunnies who are in some way different from them, and this is sad because they are all just bunnies. Everybunny is different on the outside in various ways, and that should be celebrated, but punk-ass bunnies don't see that. Gratefully, Snow was not a punk-ass bunny.

Snow met Tija the first day of creator training and they bonded immediately because Snow somehow knew and directly employed the Security Spell with Tija. Snow saw the Fear Tija had about training, then saw more than Tija's Fear, and made Tija feel less afraid by comforting Tija and making Tija laugh. A lot. Snow simply wanted Tija to feel safe and required nothing in return. This precious gift at such a vulnerable time made Tija trust Snow.

They were Friends, and remained Friends throughout their time in creator training and after, seeing each other clearer and clearer as time went on. They were so close, in fact, that some bunnies questioned if they were dining together. But, Tija liked rhubarb and Snow was a carrot connoisseur. Still, they were as close as Friends could be.

Because of this closeness, as Tija's Love and commitment to Tob grew, so did Snow's disdain and distrust for Tob. Snow, along with Tija's other Friends, simply could not understand how Tija could be so full of light and happiness when around them and then immediately seem small, subdued, and dejected when Tob was around. It almost seemed that in order for Tob to shine, Tija needed to dim.

Throughout the time with Tob, Tija developed three basic modes of existence:

1.) Tija with Tob.

2.) Tija with others.

3.) Tija in make-believe.

Now, this third mode was becoming more and more complicated because of the Fear levels in the first, and the sometimes drastic changes that needed to occur when transitioning from the first to the second. Still, always striving for excellence, Tija was determined to figure all of this out.

Alright, Teej, here's the plan for success! I know, Tob is still hurting you from time to time, but Tob clearly explains how these episodes are actually your fault. Honestly, I think we both know that these things would not be happening if you could

just get the Spell of Perfection right, but whatever.
Here's the plan: When you are with Tob, use the
Spell of Perfection the best you can to make Tob
happy, and if Tob is ever unhappy, use the Fear-
Avoidance Spell so Tob's unhappiness doesn't hurt
you as much. Then, when you're with other
bunnies, you just get reckless with that Security
Spell; that seems to make you and other bunnies
happy. As for make-believe...here's the thing, Teej,
I'm not really sure why you're foolin' with this
make-believe shit. I mean, you're not very good at
it. Thankfully, Tob was nice enough to tell you!
But, you seem to still wanna do it, so...go ahead.

And so, as Tija continued trying to master the Spell of Perfection, it became very adept at passing through these three basic modes of existence. So adept that almost everybunny around Tija had no idea the level of acrobatics Tija had to perform. Tija became so good at going in and out of modes that something magical occurred: Tija finally learned how to lie. It did not quite know how to feel about this magic; it knew that it was raised to never lie, and that was always pretty easy since there was seldom reason to lie. But now, between avoiding Tob's wrath and hiding pain from others, Tija felt it had very good reason to get very good at lying.

However, the Spell of Deceit had drawbacks. Because Tob's Fear fed off of Tija's growing Fear, Tob's ability to catch Tija in a lie was improving, even if the lie was told to assuage Tob. This caused Tob to become even more angry with Tija, which made Tija want to get even better at the Spell of Deceit, while also trying to conquer the Spell of Perfection, while also sharpening the Fear-Avoidance Spell so Tob could shine, while also employing the Security Spell with others so they too could be happy!

Tija was frequently exhausted. Tija's bunny body began to change as the Fear-Avoidance Spell caused Tija more physical pain. Tija's fur began to fall out in certain spots, so it trimmed its fur very short. Tija spoke with less certainty, and make-believe, the first real Joy of Tija's life, became less enjoyable. And Snow saw all of this.

Unlike some other bunnies in Tija's life, Snow was a Friend Tija could not hide from.

"What are you doing?" Snow asked one day while at Tija's home. "I Love you, Tija. But I do not Love who you become around Tob."

"It's not Tob's fault! It's me. I just can't seem to get it right," Tija replied.

"I don't think that's True," Snow persisted.

"No!" fired Tija, "It really is me. Tob is right. I'm selfish and needy and, look at me, I'm far from a cute bunny. It's a wonder Tob even wants to be with me at all. And I've become a liar! I really am an unloveable bunny, and somehow Tob still Loves me, so the least I can do is Love Tob the way it wants."

Snow did not know what to say, until it knew what to say. "But, what do you want, Tija?"

Tija paused a moment and thought, *I just want to be happy.* And Tija said, "I just want Tob to be happy." Snow looked into Tija's eyes and saw nothing but big, beautiful, brown bunny pupils absolutely filled with Fear.

Before Snow could speak, they heard Tob's keys in Tija's door. "Oh hey, Snow! How are ya?" greeted Tob with a brilliant smile. Tija quickly responded before Snow could even think. "Snow was just heading to work, stopped by on the way. I'll see ya later this week!" Tija said to Snow, smiling hard and holding the door open for Snow to leave. Aghast, Snow could only stare at Tija. Tija smiled insistently as Snow slowly left. Tija swiftly closed the door.

"That Snow is an odd bunny," said Tob. Tija let out something close to a laugh in response and began to busy itself by tidying up the kitchen. With Tija's back turned in activity, Tob approached Tija in a way that looked like Love and put its arms around Tija, which made Tija smile. *Perhaps this will be one of the good days!* "Ya know," Tob singsonged while embracing Tija, "Now would be a great time for rhubarb. We haven't had any in a while."

Tija smiled. "You are quite right! But I do have to go to work in a bit, so maybe we'll have some later tonight."

"I'll be too tired later tonight. Can't we have some now?" Tob pleaded while starting to tickle Tija.

Tija did not like to be tickled but allowed it,
grateful for the mood Tob was in.

"How about this?" bargained Tija. "We'll get up
early tomorrow and have some fresh, delicious
rhubarb first thing!"

Tob released Tija. "Why do you always do this?"
Tob asked in quiet frustration. "Every time I have a
good day and want to spend time with you and
have some rhubarb, you make some selfish excuse
to have it on your terms."

"Oh, no! That's not what I meant at all!" Tija said,
desperately trying to save the moment. "I just
meant that since I have to leave soon, we'd have
more time to actually enjoy some rhubarb in the
morning. That's all!" Tob began to silently pace,
becoming angrier with each step. Tija immediately

employed the Security Spell and tried the Spell of Perfection simultaneously. "I just enjoy rhubarb with you so much that I want to make sure that everything is exactly right!" Tija said with a smile while taking Tob's paw. Tob jerked away.

"So here we are back to everything being about you. Great!" shot Tob.

Tija quickly employed the Fear-Avoidance Spell. "No! No, it's not about me at all! I'm happy you even want to have rhubarb with me. I know how upset I can make you and I am sorry. That's exactly why I want us to have the time to enjoy the rhubarb! I'm sorry, Tob."

Tob let out a deep sigh. "I know. I know you're sorry. I just don't know how many apologies for your selfishness I can take." Tob slumped down in a kitchen chair, forcing tears to well up in its eyes. Tija, overcome with shame, had no idea what to do nor say. "Do you even really love me?" Tob asked, searching Tija's face. Tija was so filled with Fear by that question it couldn't see anything in Tob's eyes. Tija could hardly see anything at all.

"Of course I do! Of course I love you, Tob!" cried Tija, falling to Tob's feet. "I love you so much and I know I don't deserve you. I promise I can be better!"

"Then why can't we have rhubarb right now?" Tob barked. "If you love me, then prove to me that you are not this selfish, ogre of a bunny and let me have some rhubarb!"

There was a moment of silence without breath.

It is True that Tija enjoyed rhubarb. It is True that Tija did not have time for rhubarb right now. It is True that in the emotional turns of the previous few minutes, Tija had absolutely no appetite for rhubarb. Tob wanted rhubarb. Tija Loved Tob. Tob made it perfectly clear that if Tija really Loved Tob, Tija would need to prove it in this moment.

That afternoon, Tijabab embarked on a new make-believe journey that took its mind away from the kitchen, away from the flat, away from the building. Tija went away.

Tob had rhubarb.

Big T and Bab

Chapter Six
Love and Fear cannot coexist.

Big T and Bab were just about the best

parents a bunny could ask for. No bunny parent is

perfect and all bunnies make mistakes, but as far as

Love and Wisdom were concerned, they made sure

Tija received as much as possible. They also made

sure to take good care of each other. So, when Big

T got sick, Bab, along with other Family members,

continued to do what they had always done and

made sure Big T had everything it needed.

However, the task of leading all of this was

sometimes too much for Bab, and more help

became necessary. Tija came home as often as it

could to help. Most of that help involved taking Big T where it needed to go, but also keeping Big T's Spirit up.

Big T was exceedingly proud of its baby bunny and told everybunny it saw just how proud of Tija it was. When Tija was younger, it used to feel embarrassed about how Big T's chest would swell with pride while going on and on about the smallest thing Tija did, but lately, Tija was just glad to see this old bunny having some Joy. It wasn't that Tija was doing anything worth bragging about, quite the contrary. Tija already graduated from creator training, but in the few years since, Tija was barely creating anything and making very little money. Whatever money Tija did make was spent barely supporting itself and Tob. Still, Big T was simply over the moon about Tijabab and refused to be silenced.

During one visit home, Bab asked Tija to join on a walk through the garden while Big T napped. Bab was becoming concerned about Tija with each visit, noticing changes in Tija's body and voice over the years. Bab also noticed Tija becoming terse and gruff with Family and other bunnies who meant no harm whatsoever.

"Tijabab," Bab began as they wandered through the weigela, "have you been feeling well?"

"Yeah, I'm fine," mumbled Tija, staring at the ground.

Bab continued, "I have seen your Spirit change as of late. You seem-", Bab did not quite know what to say, until it knew what to say. Bab stopped and looked at Tija, "You seem to have a general anger about you most of the time. And when the anger is not there, your Spirit seems burdened with a mantle of melancholy." Bab lifted Tija's head, looked into Tija's eyes, and smiled. "I really miss my cute little bunny." Tija gently removed Bab's paw and said just as gently, "I'm not your cute little bunny anymore," and began to walk away.

"Excuse me!" Bab snapped, quickly turning Tija back around. "First of all, you will never turn your back and walk away from me as long as you live. Is that clear?" Before Tija could respond, Bab continued. "Secondly, you may not feel cute and you may not be little, but as long as you are a bunny, you are mine and that will never change. Is

THAT clear?" Tija, speechless, simply nodded. "Now tell me," demanded Bab, "what has been going on with you?"

Tija's thoughts began to race! *You cannot tell Bab. You can't, Teej! It will never understand the hurt or the taking of rhubarb or how you've become a lying ogre of a bunny who can't do anything right. It'll just hate you. And Big T?! Come on! The rabbit's already sick. It's got enough to deal with. It does not need its baby bunny running home for help!*

Tija stood and stared at Bab- stared and stared and stared and could not say one word. Fear had stolen Tija's voice. Bab put its paws on Tija's shoulders, frightened at the sight of Tija's Fear-filled eyes. Tija collapsed! Tija was much bigger than Bab, and Bab was not prepared to support Tija's full weight, so they both hit the ground. Tija began to shake uncontrollably, gasping for air between rivers of tears. Bab desperately tried to still Tija's bunny body while also trying to not cause more harm, bewildered by what could have possibly caused such a sudden and violent attack! Bab managed to put a soothing paw on Tija's head. In time, Tija's body quieted, and the two bunnies laid on the ground, breathing amid hushed tears as Bab held Tija tight. After an hour- or maybe only a minute, Tija stood up.

"I'm sorry," Tija whispered. "I'm...I'm sorry. I'm fine, though." Tija walked away, leaving a very worried and baffled Bab still sitting on the garden ground.

"I Love you!" Bab cried out to it's baby. Tija stopped and turned to its parent, nearly exploding with a Fear so great that Bab could see it even with the distance between them. Bab rose and ran to Tija. "I Love you, Tija. I don't know what happens when you are not here, but I need you to know that Love is here. This Fear you are bringing from out there is killing you and whatever is out there cannot be Love because it is impossible for Love and Fear to live together."

"I'm fine!" cried Tija, trying in vain to escape Bab's gaze.

"You may be fine with all that Fear in you, but I am not!" declared Bab as it grabbed Tija's paw and all but dragged Tija back into the house.

Bab flung open the side door, shot up the steps with Tija still in tow, and practically threw Tija in the chair beside Big T's bed. "Oh! Oh my- what's the matter?" asked a suddenly awakened Big T. "Look into Tija's eyes!" commanded Bab. Big T sat up in the bed and looked into Tija's eyes, then let out a long whistle. "Well!" Big T exclaimed, "I haven't seen eyes like that since you were seven! You got a big Fear situation, huh?"

Tija could not believe how Big T was able to immediately see its Fear. *How?* Tija thought. *I've been learning how to disguise it better! I've gotten*

almost as good as... "Tob," Tija whispered aloud.

"Tob," Big T replied.

Tija felt as if its mind was on fire. *Teej, No! Holy*

shit, you can't tell Big T! Teej! I swear to- no! Do

not do this, Teej.

"Is Tob the one giving you all this Fear?"

asked Big T.

Stop right now, Teej! I mean, right now!! Don't be

a stupid bunny and ruin home too! You've already

ruined everything else- what the actual fuck was

that in the garden!? All that crying and thrashing

around- you looked like a goddamn r-

"ENOUGH!!!" Tija cried.

There was silence.

"Do give us a moment, won't you?" Big T quietly requested from its spouse. Bab could only oblige, and left the room to find some well-deserved party punch.

...

"I..."

...

"it..."

...help.

"I need help," Tija finally said.

"Alright, Tijabab," said Big T. "I want you to think back to what I told you about Fear when you were seven."

"But I'm not seven anymore!" Tija sobbed. "I'm not seven and this isn't a dream! This is real and this is Love and-"

"No. No, no, no," Big T shook its head. "This may be many things, my beautiful bunny, but it is not Love. Not if all that Fear is surrounding it. No. Love and Fear cannot coexist."

"That's exactly what Bab said," Tija replied.

"Well, you should listen. Bab knows what it's talking about," Big T continued. "Now, no bunny is a bad bunny, but you put enough Fear in a bunny and that Fear will morph it into something out-of-this-world bad! I'm sure there are a lot of wonderful things about Tob, but Tob's Fear? Bun, Tob's Fear will eventually kill you if you let it. And, if Tob kills you, then I'll have to kill Tob, then Tob's Family will kill me, and then you've got a whole world problem! Now do you think this world needs more problems?" Big T chuckled.

"No." Tija said. "But, what do I do when I see Tob again?"

Big T paused for a moment, then slowly swung its legs out of the bed so it was sitting face-to-face with Tija. "Here's where it gets difficult, Tijabab. Sadly, if this Tob character is giving you this much Fear, there must be a whole bunch of

Fear in Tob. When a bunny is that far gone into Fear, you have to let that bunny go. I know you care for Tob a great deal, but Tob cannot Love you nor anybunny truly with all that Fear inside. You have to let Tob go and...hope. Hope Tob finds what it needs. Hope Tob finds the bunny it needs- but that bunny ain't you. Not now. Not ever. Do you understand?"

Tija exhaled, "I do...but I just don't actually know how to let Tob go." Big T smiled a bit. "You do, Tijabab. Tackle the Fear within you, then remove the Fear around you- employ the spell."

Tija

__Chapter Seven__

Freedom is a journey.

When embarking on a journey to Freedom,

one must understand a few things:

1.) Guide your thoughts.

   If Fear is controlling your thoughts, they

will sound mean and nasty. They will speak

negatively of you, and take every opportunity to

make you feel shame. Fear-controlled thoughts

will change your perception, image, ideas, ideals,

and sense of worth. This is why it is paramount to

guide your thoughts with Love. As Fear and Love

cannot coexist, and Love walks in tandem with

Truth, Love is essential to Freedom.

2). Despite what was, look at what is.

Far too often we can remain in situations or entertain individuals who formerly edified, but currently corrode our lives. We alone are responsible for identifying the corrosion, and recognizing the specific damage it causes. If the damage is ignored, then our allegiance to the situation and/or individual must be withdrawn, lest we be destroyed.

3.) Keep what you can, but get what you need.

Everything has a price and some things may be irreplaceable, but if you are in a spiritual prison, there is no price too high for Freedom. If it won't cost you everything, then definitely take all you can with you. But, if all you can take is you, that is all you need.

***

It would be glorious if Tijabab became Free the moment it returned from Big T and Bab's, but that is not True. Ideally, a bunny would Free itself from a bad situation, but sadly, for many bunnies, the first revelation is not enough. It would take Tija four hundred and ninety-nine more days and nights to learn how to guide its thoughts, see what is, and get what it needed. It would take O.G.B. rescuing Tija when Tob's Fear nearly took Tija's life. It would take Snow pleading with Tija to stop making excuses for Tob's behavior and leave an increasingly dangerous situation. It would take Tija failing at every spell it learned while with Tob. But, by the five hundredth night, Tija was finally ready to make itself Free.

It was the night of Tija's birthday, and Tob planned a special surprise for Tija. Tija did not exactly hurry home to their shared first-floor flat after work, unsure of what this could possibly mean. After a gift Tija never asked for and a card Tija did not believe, Tob presented Tija with a small box. Tob smiled brightly. "I want us to share our lives, Tija. Forever." It was a proposal. A commitment. A symbol of Love and devotion the likes of which anybunny would be overjoyed to receive.

"This..." Tija murmured to a kneeling, beaming Tob who gently whispered, "Oh, please say yes."

Tija did not know what to say...until it knew what to say. Tija stood up tall, took a deep breath, and said with quiet deliberate sternness, "You get the fuck outta here."

Speak the Truth, Tijabab.

"This is not Love. Love would not hurt me the way you have hurt me."

Speak the Truth, Tijabab. I Love You.

"I may not be everything I want to be, but I no longer believe I am what you say. I no longer want this. I no longer want you, and I don't care what you say or do or what you want to believe. This will not go on!"

Tob froze. Tija took advantage of this opportunity, headed briskly to the bedroom, locked the door, grabbed a bag, and began stuffing it with everything essential.

"TIJA!" Tob's shock had broken and was replaced with utter fury. Tob raced to the locked bedroom door screaming, its fists flailing to break the door down. Tija ran for the bureau and pushed it in front of the door, then immediately started on a second bag. Tob's Fear was in complete control of Tob's body, fortifying it with enough rageful strength to punch through the door and start ripping pieces of wood from the frame to get to

Tija. From above the bureau between them, Tija caught a glimpse of Tob's eyes. In them, Tija saw the full face of Fear. *It looks just like the night terrors! Tija, you have to use the spell! You must!!*

"Fear!" Tija commanded. "You get the fuck outta here!!!"

Tob was almost through the door and could easily knock down the bureau. There was no time to waste! In a flash, Tija opened the bedroom window, threw the two bags onto the pavement, leapt out the window, and closed it behind. And then, Tija ran! Tija ran faster than any rabbit had ever run. With a bag in each paw, Tija didn't care what it was wearing or how it looked; the only thing on Tija's mind was Freedom!

In the months ahead, Tija stayed with Snow or another beautiful Friend not well-known by Tob. Tija and Tob communicated only on matters involving shared property, and almost always by letter. Tob and Tob's fear found fun and interesting ways to spin the dissolution of the relationship, casting Tija in the role of all sorts of villains. None of this was True, of course, but if that is what Tob felt it needed to do, Tija had absolutely no problem allowing anybun to believe whatever they wanted. The Truth is the Truth, and that is just a point of fact.

Tijabab

Chapter Eight

Forgiveness is like water. Bathe in it!

It is often inconvenient to guide one's thoughts with Love and walk in Love when it comes to those who have brought fear into your life. However, the best way Tija found to deal with any talk of Tob was with modifications to the known spells.

Tija started with the Spell to Send Fear Away, reducing it to a simple "No." Saying "No." is a wonderful thing as it is both complete within itself and it is final. "No." means "No." and it is not an invitation for further discourse. Yet, there were times this spell proved insufficient for some, so Tija made a few changes to the Fear- Avoidance Spell. Tija would no longer use it to make itself smaller and invariably uncomfortable; rather, Tija would use the spell to eliminate discussion altogether. "I am sure Tob is doing whatever it is Tob needs to do with whomever Tob needs to do that with, and I hope everybunny is happy with whatever is going on," Tija frequently and snarkily said. Tija then immediately employed the Security Spell to turn the conversation toward the positive and uplifting.

As for the Spell of Perfection and the Spell of Deceit, Tija quickly learned that they are stupid, pointless, ridiculous lies that must never be believed. Ever.

While this mode of operation served Tija in the beginning of Freedom, it proved to be somewhat binding at the same time. *I do not fully understand,* Tija would think. *We are safer and happier, but it does seem that we are having to distract focus away from Tob a lot...almost as if Tob still has some sort of power over us. The spells work with other bunnies, but I am not sure if we feel better when we use them.* Tija did not know exactly what it was feeling lately, but was determined to figure it out. *We are happy to be away from harm. We are happy to feel safe. We are confident in what to look out for to stay safe:*

1.) Do not trust anybun who seeks to diminish you.

2.) Always trust your gut.

3.) Know that if it involves fear, it cannot be Love.

4.) If you are not walking in Love with yourself,
beware who comes along to walk with you.

5.) If you are not being Loved for who you are,
then you are not being Loved at all.

6.) Love and fear cannot coexist.

7.) Love and Truth must coexist.

What could be missing? What is keeping us from truly enjoying Freedom?

"Forgiveness.", Tija said to itself one night a few years later. The very idea of it almost made Tija immediately laugh out loud. But Tija's Love-guided thoughts would not let that word go.

For months Tija wrestled with it- *Forgiveness. Forgiveness. Forgiveness.* -until finally, Tija could not avoid it any longer. "Alright! Fine. You keep saying this and I am, frankly, sick of hearing about it so... fine. I Forgive that goddamn rabbit Tob! I Forgive Tob for all the fucked-up shit Tob did! Now, please leave me alone about it!"

Oh, Tijabab. We are nowhere near discussing Tob.

"Well then...I just don't understand. Why have you been repeating 'Forgiveness' so much?"

Tija, you need to Forgive yourself for thinking you ever deserved those awful things. Forgive yourself for letting fear guide your mind and words and actions. Forgive yourself for thinking that this type of behavior was acceptable, let alone anything remotely close to Love. Fear is a liar, Tija, but fear is not deaf. Fear can hear how you speak to others, and it can also hear how you speak to yourself. And if you are speaking about Tob with words of anger or bitterness or shame- Tija, those are fear's best disguises. It recognizes those things and will start to see the familiarity as an invitation. The next thing you know, you are in another similar

situation. It may not escalate to the levels it did

with Tob, but it will be a fear situation. We need no

more of those.

Tijabab was silent for days. In time, the

Love that guided Tija's thoughts began to guide

Tija's words. These words were devoid of sarcasm

or jest; they were direct and deliberate. "Tijabab,"

it said to itself, "I Love you. And, because I Love

you, I want you to stay in and enjoy Freedom. I

Forgive you for ever believing you deserved those

awful things. You are worthy of Good Love, and

even if nobunny shares that with you, you are

allowed nothing less within yourself."

Tijabab found itself thinking or saying words like this whenever any mention of Tob occurred in the coming years, and although these brief internal excursions seemed odd, they were helpful. There was no fanfare nor opulently cathartic moments necessarily, but Tija's heartbeat didn't change tempo as much. Breathing became easier. There was less spell work. And the most interesting, unexplainable, and unexpected thing occurred: Tija's fur, although still short and a bit patchy from the years before, became softer. Tija found a softness it hadn't felt since childhood. The Love-guided thoughts brought Forgiveness like water, and the more Tija bathed in it, the softer Tija became.

This is not to say there were not days Tija neglected this water, but Tija soon learned that Forgiveness was not so much a decision as it was a practice, one that became easier as time went on. And with each Forgiveness, Tija was made clean and felt more and more like a soft, beautiful bunny.

***

There were plenty more adventures and odysseys, trials and tribulations for Tijabab, but there would never again be a journey like this one: the journey from fear to Freedom. Tija vowed to never have contact with Tob again and was eventually able to Forgive Tob for an apology Tija never received, nor required. Big T and Bab, O.G.B., Snow, and all of Tija's Friends were overjoyed whenever they saw Tija because they now recognized the beautiful bunny they knew and Loved. Tija's Spirit and body began to heal, and Tija found it could not only enjoy rhubarb again, but in the absence of fear and shame, it was more delicious than Tija ever imagined! Tijabab in Freedom was once again Secure. Most importantly, Tija learned that when Love guided its thoughts, words, and actions, it was able to truly thrive. Love taught Tija spells and lessons far more advanced and helpful than fear ever could.

As for make-believe, Tija found a renewed Joy! Except now make-believe was no longer

Tija's only escape to fearlessness. Tija's Joy became a space for Truth.

The End

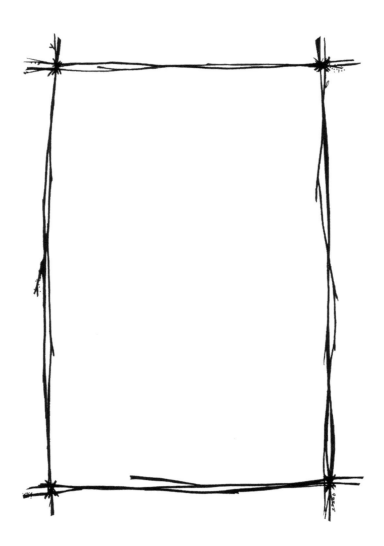

Epilogue

The last time Tijabab would ever see Big T's eyes, they were smiling. Big T's were the only eyes in the room completely without fear. "It's alright, Tija," Big T said. "End of life is still life...it's just the end. You live and then you die. But, as long as you learn how to live Free, you do not have to fear the end. Understand?"

Tija understood as much as a twenty-seven-year-old bunny could.

"Yes."

Acknowledgements

Wendy Bable

Andy Bigelow

Stephfond Brunson

Brittany Campbell

Lee Colston II

Briana Cox

Kirk Duncan

Jesediah

Ema Kamara

Shaun Kane

Ben Michael

Malika Oyetimein

About the Illustrator

Chris Bresky is an author, playwright, illustrator, and performer. He has been inspired by the delightfully twisted works of Edward Gorey, Jim Henson, Shel Silverstein, and Roald Dahl. Mr. Bresky currently works at Adler Planetarium in Chicago where he invents creative ways for students to engage with science. He is kept grounded by his wife, Moriah, and his daughter/ baby dragon named Ruby.

Photographer: Wade Berger

Fuck the patriarchy.

Made in the USA
Columbia, SC
06 November 2018